# FLUSH!
## AND 37 ESSENTIAL HOUSE RULES

Written and illustrated
by Mrs Wordsmith

# AH,

It's like a crash test course for the rest of kids' lives. It's a safe place where they can test the boundaries and learn how to operate before they're let loose on the outside world.

That's why house rules are so important. They help kids learn to self-regulate and take responsibility for themselves, laying the foundations for school and beyond.

We created Flush! to help make this stage in kids' learning as hilariously fun and memorable as possible.

Good luck. This could get messy.

# House Contract

LOVE IS THE SECRET TO A
HAPPY HOME, BUT A FEW RULES
ALSO HELP.

WE PROMISE TO LIVE BY THESE
37 HOUSE RULES. SOME OF THEM
ARE SMALL. SOME OF THEM ARE EPIC.

TOGETHER WE CAN MAKE OUR HOME
A BETTER, CLEANER, SMARTER,
AND MORE LOVING PLACE TO LIVE.

SIGNED BY:

X

_____        _____

_____        _____

_____        _____

OZ

YIN & YANG

MEET THE

# FAMILY

BUNNYMOON

BARKSY

BOGART

PLATO

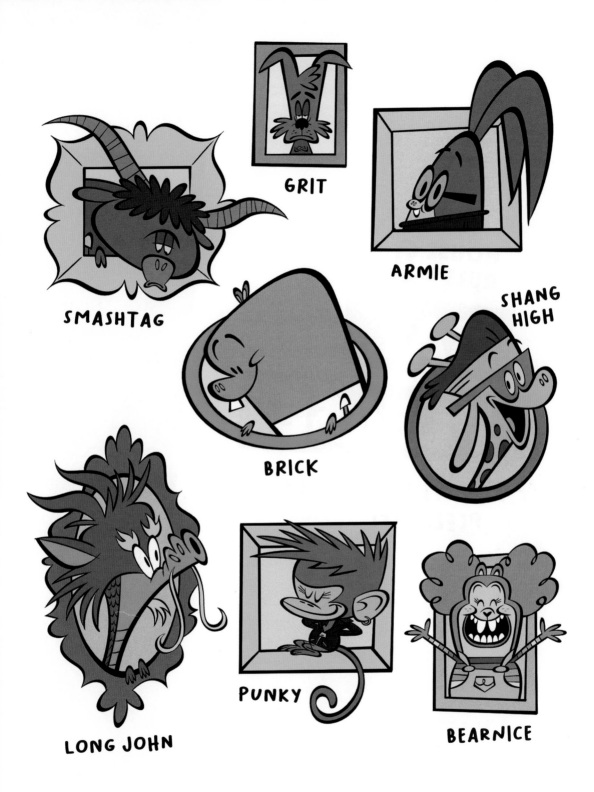

GRIT

ARMIE

SMASHTAG

SHANG HIGH

BRICK

LONG JOHN

PUNKY

BEARNICE

# HOUSE RULE # 1

## SAY PLEASE

ALWAYS SAY PLEASE.
PLEEAASE!

# desire

*v.* to want something
very badly

# HOUSE RULE # 2

## SAY THANK YOU

IT FEELS GOOD
TO SAY THANK YOU.

**grateful**

*adj.* feeling thankful

# HOUSE RULE # 3

## SHARE

#SHARINGISCARING

**insensitive**

*adj.* not thinking about
someone else's feelings

# HOUSE RULE # 4

## SMILE

**reminisce**

*v.* to enjoy remembering past events

# HOUSE RULE # 5

# LISTEN

SHOW ME A SIGN
THAT YOU ARE
LISTENING.

ANY SIGNAL,
NO MATTER HOW WEAK,
WILL DO.

## oblivious

*adj.* completely unaware
of what is happening
around you

# HOUSE RULE # 6

# FIND IT YOURSELF

**pinpoint**

*v.* find or identify something very precisely

# HOUSE RULE # 1

## GO
## OUTSIDE

### AT LEAST ONCE A DAY.

# HOUSE RULE # 8

## SCOOP
## THE
## POOP

WE ALL
WALK THE POOCH.

**inadequate**

*adj.* when something isn't
enough for the job

HOUSE
RULE # **9**

# LAYER

# UP

DRESS FOR THE
SEASON YOU'VE
GOT.

NOT THE ONE
YOU WANT.

## frostbitten

*adj.* hurt or injured
because it's so cold

**HOUSE RULE # 10**

# SHOES OFF

YO, COSMIC ANGEL!
LEAVE YOUR WINGS
AT THE DOOR.

**respect**

*v.* to treat people and places politely and with appreciation

## HOUSE RULE # 11

## HANG

## IT

## UP

**dangle**

*v.* hang or swing

# HOUSE RULE # 12

# BREATHE

BREATHE IN
ALL THE GOOD.

BLOW AWAY
THE BAD.

**mindful**

*adj.* focusing on the
present and taking
a deep breath

# HOUSE RULE # 13

## REMEMBER TO RECHARGE

tenderness

*n.* warmth, gentleness, and affection

# HOUSE RULE # 14

## POWER OFF

### YOUR GAME.

AND
POWER UP
YOUR
BRAIN.

**inspire**

*v.* to fill your head
with new ideas

# HOUSE RULE # 15

# USE YOUR BRAIN

## WHAT IF GOOGLE WAS DELETED?

**contemplate**

*v.* to think about something very deeply

# HOUSE RULE # 16

# READ

READ MINDS.

WORD-O's

READ CEREAL BOXES.

READ
LIPS.

READ
BOOKS.

**avid**

*adj.* enthusiastic
and interested

# HOUSE RULE # 17

## DO IT YOURSELF

IF YOU CAN DREAM IT,
YOU CAN MAKE IT.

**design**

*v.* to plan how something
should be made

HOUSE
RULE # **18**

# KISS

## AND

# GO

Kiss & Fly

KISS YOUR FAMILY
BEFORE YOU LEAVE
THE HOUSE.

## appreciate

*v.* to value or be thankful
for something

# HOUSE RULE # 19

## LET

## IT

## OUT

**bawl**

*v.* to cry with long, emotional sobs

HOUSE RULE # 20

# TIDY UP

IT'S CALLED THE LIVING ROOM, NOT THE LEAVE-YOUR-MESS-EVERYWHERE ROOM.

**chaos**

*n.* total confusion and disorder

# HOUSE RULE # 21

## WASH
### YOUR
## HANDS

WHO INVITED THE GERMSES TO DINNER?

**filthy**

*adj.* disgustingly dirty

# HOUSE RULE # 22

## PUT
### IT
## AWAY

iPHONE

iPAD

**covert**

*adj.* secret, stealthy, or hidden

# HOUSE RULE # 23
## EAT UP

THERE ARE TWO OPTIONS
FOR DINNER:

   1. TAKE IT

   2. LEAVE IT

**fussy**

*adj.* someone who only
likes certain things

# HOUSE RULE # 24

## DOUGH

## NOT

...CHEW WITH
YOUR MOUTH
OPEN.

# overambitious

*adj.* trying to do something
that's far too difficult

# HOUSE RULE # 25

## KEEP IT CLEAN

THERE ARE BETTER WORDS THAN "@&%!!"

**courteous**

*adj.* respectful of others

HOUSE RULE # **26**

# DO

## YOUR

# HOMEWORK

NO EXCUSES.

**distraction**

*n.* something that stops you from concentrating

HOUSE RULE # 27

# SHUT THE FRIDGE

THE SALAD IS UNDRESSED.

## scandalous

*adj.* outrageous
and shocking

# HOUSE RULE # 28

# CLEAR

## THE

## TABLE

AND HELP WITH
THE DISHES.

**efficient**

*adj.* quick and effective

# HOUSE RULE # 29

# REDUCE!
# REUSE!
# RECYCLE!

LET NOTHING GO TO WASTE.

## sustainable

*adj.* less bad for
the environment

HOUSE
RULE #30

# SWITCH

# OFF

### THE

# LIGHTS

ALL THE BEST NINJAS
TRAIN IN
THE DARK.

## stealthy

*adj.* quiet and careful so that
nobody sees you

HOUSE RULE # **31**

# USE A BATH MAT

# THE BATHROOM FLOOR IS NOT A WATER PARK.

## slippery

*adj.* too wet or slimy
to hold or stand on

# HOUSE RULE # 32

## PICK

## IT

## UP

THE BATHROOM FLOOR
IS NOT THE WILD TOWEL'S
NATURAL HABITAT.

**damp**

*adj.* slightly wet

# HOUSE RULE # 33

## NO
## DOG
## BREATH

BRUSH YOUR TEETH
FOR TWO MINUTES
TWICE DAILY.

**30 SECONDS...**

**60 SECONDS...**

**120 SECONDS.**

## diligent

*adj.* done in a careful and serious way

# HOUSE RULE # 34

# REPLACE
# THE
# TOILET
# PAPER

**flustered**

*adj.* upset and confused

# HOUSE RULE # 35

## FLUSH

### OR ELSE YOUR POO MIGHT ESCAPE

HOUSE
RULE # 36

BEDTIME
MEANS
BEDTIME

"WHEN I SAY BEDTIME,

YOU SAY GOODNIGHT!"

**compelling**

*adj.* persuasive or hard to resist

# HOUSE RULE # 37

# FOLLOW

## YOUR

# HEART

AND LOVE
FROM YOUR HEAD
TO YOUR TAIL.

## exceptional

*adj.* special or extraordinary

AND FINALLY,

HOUSE RULE # 38

# PARENTS HAVE RULES TOO

GET OFF YOUR PHONE!

STOP TRYING TO MAKE ME LIKE YOUR TERRIBLE MUSIC.

NO PHOTOS PLEASE.

DON'T DANCE IN PUBLIC. EVER.

GIVE ME HUGS.

## YOU NEED TO KNOW THE RULES...

When you stay quiet in order to listen to others, wait for your turn, or share a toy with a friend, you are using self-regulation. Kids who can regulate their emotions are better prepared to cope with challenging situations, whether you need to concentrate on a difficult test, deal with disappointing news, or manage a complex relationship.

## ...TO BREAK THE RULES

Kids who can think for themselves and who respect their homes and the people around them go on to do unexpected and incredible things. Flush! provides you with the rules you need to become an independent thinker, a visionary, and even a renegade.

# MADE WITH LOVE BY

**Editor-in-Chief**
Sofia Fenichell

**Researcher**
Eleni Savva

**Artists**
Daniel Permutt
Nicolò Mereu
Phillip Mamuyac
Aghnia Mardiyah
Brett Coulson

**Writers**
Mark Holland
Tatiana Barnes
Sawyer Eaton
Amelia Mehra

**Designers**
Lady San Pedro
James Sales